OPERATION:
Puppy Patrol

Latoya Britt
Illustrated by Gracie Cole

Dedication:

This book is dedicated to my firstborn son, Caleb.
You are my dream come true, literally.
Ase' Ase'

Kizzy quietly walks into her father's office, tiptoeing so she doesn't disturb him while he's on the phone. She leans in closely and peers over his shoulder, just as he is finishing up his conversation.

"I'll see you tomorrow, " General Brown takes off his glasses and hangs up the phone. "Daddy, are you going on another top secret mission? Where are we going this time?" Kizzy asks her dad excitedly, tapping her fingers on his desk playfully. "Well, Kizzy," replies General Brown, "it looks like we're off again. I have to meet with the King of Thailand. We won't be able to spend a lot of time together, but you'll be staying with close friends of mine while we're there. I think you'll enjoy your time with them, they have a daughter your age."

"This trip sounds like it's gonna be a lot of fun! I wonder what my new friend will be like. When do we leave, Daddy?" Kizzy asks, dancing around the room.

"Our flight leaves in the morning, so you should go upstairs and start packing. We'll be there for a week. Oh yeah, make sure you pack your raincoat. It rains a lot in Thailand," General Brown tells Kizzy.

The next day, Kizzy and her dad leave for Thailand. Kizzy sleeps most of the plane ride, but is excited by the size of the International Airport. She is most intrigued by the Thai language and whispers to her dad that it sounds like everyone is singing when they speak, because their voices are soft and friendly, including the men.

Her excitement continues and she wonders what's in store for her during her visit. After a short car ride through the busy city, they arrive at the Suwan residence in the countryside, where Kizzy will be staying for the week.

" Kizzy, the Suwans and their daughter, Nattaya, are going to make sure you have a lot of fun while I'm working. I'll be back to pick you up at that end of the week." Mr. Suwan smiles at Kizzy's dad as they shake hands.

"General, it's so good to see you. It's been years. The girls will be fine," he replies reassuringly.

"We'll be sure to call you if we need to." General Brown bows to the Suwan family, a gesture commonly used to show appreciation. Mrs. Suwan smiles at Kizzy warmly and bows in return.

The general turns and gives Kizzy a quick hug before leaving with his military personnel.

The girls head to the guest room and unpack Kizzy's things.

Kizzy watches as Nattaya takes off her shoes and puts on a pair of slippers by the front door. Nattaya tells Kizzy to take off her shoes and points to another pair of slippers for her to put on.

As they begin to talk, Kizzy notices that Nattaya seems sad.

"What's the matter?" Kizzy asks her new friend.

"I just saw on the news that the King's dog is missing. I've never had a dog before, but I bet I'd be really sad if I lost him," Nattaya sighs in disbelief.

Kizzy looks at her new friend and snaps her fingers. "Hey Nattaya, I've got an idea," she says, excitedly. "If you're willing to help me, maybe we can start our own mission and find the King's dog!" she continues, following Nattaya to the guest bedroom.

Nattaya raises her eyebrows. "Wow, so you're going to find the King's dog?"

"No, *we're* going to find the King's dog," Kizzy smiles at Nattaya. "We'll figure it out together, as a team! Are you in?" Kizzy asks Nattaya, reaching out her hand to seal the deal.

"I'm in!" Nattaya replies, as she grabs Kizzy's hand, sealing their friendship.

After Kizzy gets settled in, the girls get right to business.

"Ok, so the first step in solving any mystery is to list all of your facts. We know the dog's name right?" Kizzy asks Nattaya, as she looks through her book bag for something to write with. "Yes. It's Chompoo," Nattaya replies. "Do we have an idea of what the dog looks like?" Kizzy asks as she writes in her journal. "Yes," Nattaya explains to Kizzy. "Chompoo is really small, with brown and tan fur. I even have a picture of him that I took at a parade." Nattaya pulls a box full of photos from under her bed. "Here it is. I found it!" she says.

She shows Kizzy her picture of Chompoo.

"Oh yea, I almost forgot," Nattaya exclaims. "Chompoo wears a special tag that looks like the Thailand flag!" "This is perfect!" Kizzy squeals as she looks closely at Nattaya's picture. "We have enough information to begin our investigation. Where should we start?", she asks. "We'll start looking near the Floating Market to see if we can find any clues. Maybe someone has seen him since he went missing." Nattaya answers. "You've had a long flight Kizzy, get some rest and we'll start our search after breakfast tomorrow."

The next day, Kizzy and Nattaya question everyone at the Floating Market.

First, they ask a woman selling silk scarves. They show her the picture of Chompoo and ask her if she's seen the dog. She shakes her head.

Next, they ask a man selling fish if he's seen Chompoo. He scratches his head, sighs, and also tells them no. They ask three men dressed as monks; they ask a couple selling vegetables; and they ask a man selling art.

However, no one seems to have any clues about the whereabouts of Chompoo. Feeling discouraged, they sit on a bench to enjoy some tea.

The tea shop owner notices the look on the girls' faces and asks how he can help.

"Well, we're on a mission to find the King's dog, and we haven't gathered one clue yet." Kizzy frowns as she takes another look at Nattaya's picture of Chompoo. "We've asked everyone in the market and no one has been able to help us," Nattaya adds.

The tea shop owner leans in to get a better look at the picture Nattaya is holding. He squints his eyes and points to a group of boys practicing Muay Thai, a form of martial arts, near the bridge. "It seems like the dog the boys are feeding and the one in your picture might be the same dog," the tea shop owner replies.

He flashes the girls a smile before he goes back into his shop. The girls look in the direction the store owner pointed to. To their surprise, the dog looks a lot like Chompoo!

They take off running and yelling in the boy's direction, trying to get their attention. However, the boys are too far away to notice. Once the girls finally arrive at the bridge, the boys who were once there are now gone.

"Oh no! Now what are we going to do?" Nattaya shouts. Kizzy starts tapping her foot. "Hmm," she says as she thinks aloud. "We have to figure out who those boys are and where they went. Maybe someone around here knows who they are," she says.

"Hey, Kizzy, I think we have our first clue. It must have fallen from someone's uniform," Nattaya says, beaming with excitement. She bends down to pick up a belt that is lying on the ground. "Is this part of their martial arts uniform?" Kizzy asks as Nattaya wipes dust off the belt. "Yes, look this belt has words on it." Nattaya exclaims.

Kizzy looks closely as Nattaya reads the words on the belt: *Rising Sun, School for Boys.*

"Do you know where that is?" Kizzy asks.

"I sure do! It's not too far from here, but it's getting late and it looks like it might rain soon," Nattaya yawns.

"We can go there first thing in the morning. Hopefully the rain holds off, but I'm not so sure we will be as lucky with the weather tomorrow." Nattaya says as she hands the belt to Kizzy.

Kizzy throws her arm around Nattaya and the girls run home so they won't get caught in the rain.

The next morning, Kizzy and Nattaya take off in the direction of the martial arts school. Once they arrive, they start to ask some of the students if they lost a belt to their uniform. However, no one seemed to know who the owner of the belt was. The girls' shoulders slump in discouragement. Just as they turn to leave, a teenage girl walks over to them.

"Hey," the girl says. "I'm Su. My dad owns this school and one of the boys told us that you two found a belt." Kizzy and Nattaya nod their heads in agreement. The girl continues, "If you're looking for the owner, I might be able to help you. Can I see the belt?" Su asks.

"Sure," Kizzy replies. "We were hoping to find out who the belt belongs to, because we believe the owner can help us with a very important...uhh..well, a very important..." Kizzy stutters. "A very important assignment!" Nattaya jumps in, finishing Kizzy's sentence. "We're looking for the King's dog, Chompoo, and we think the owner of the belt might be able to help us."

Su pauses and thinks for a moment. "Well, all of the belts have the student's initials on the inside. I know this because I hand sewed the initials on each belt myself." She winks at Kizzy and Nattaya as she flips the belt over to show them the initials sewn on the inside.

"See," Su remarks, "the initials on the back of this belt are 'Y.S.' which means this belt belongs to Yuri Sung. Yuri lives right around the corner from here, near the pond at the end of the street. You should hurry if you want to catch up with him. He usually does his chores in the afternoon," Su tells them. The girls squeal in excitement and thank the owner's daughter. They run off in the direction of the pond hoping to find another clue in their search for Chompoo.

20

As they run down the street, they notice a young boy in the yard, moving his arms and feet, as if he is preparing for a fight.

"Hey, Nattaya, do you think that might be Yuri Sung?" Kizzy asks.

"Yes, I think that's him. He is practicing martial arts," Nattaya replies.

The girls quickly run towards the yard to meet the young boy.

"Excuse me," Nattaya says interrupting the boy from his practice. "Are you Yuri Sung?" The boy pauses and looks at the girls curiously.

"Maybe," he responds.

"Hi. I'm Nattaya and this is my friend, Kizzy. She's from the United States. We saw you in the market yesterday and we were wondering if you lost a belt." Kizzy hands the belt to the boy.

"Hey!" Yuri exclaims. "I've been looking everywhere for this belt. I need this for my uniform," Yuri folds his arms across his chest and raises an eyebrow in confusion. "Wait a minute, how did you know my name and where to find me?" he asks them.

"We found your belt near the market yesterday. We saw the name of the school on the back of the belt and we went there earlier today looking for you. The owner's daughter told us you might be here," Nattaya explains to Yuri.

"I'm sorry for my behavior. Thank you so much. This belt really means a lot to me," Yuri tells the girls. "If there's anything I can do to return the favor, I'll be glad to help," Yuri says apologetically.

The girls look at each other and smile as Nattaya reaches for the picture of Chompoo. "Actually there is something you can help us with," Kizzy says. "When we saw you and your friends near the market yesterday, we noticed you were playing with a small dog." Kizzy points to the picture of Chompoo. "We think the dog you were playing with belongs to the King of Thailand. We were wondering if you knew where we could find the dog?" Kizzy asks Yuri . "Is the dog here?" Nattaya asks excitedly as she glances around the yard for signs of Chompoo.

"Wait, you mean the *King's missing dog*??" Yuri asks in utter disbelief. Kizzy and Nattaya both nod their heads in agreement.

Yuri continues, "I brought the dog home with me yesterday because I've always wanted a dog, but my parents wouldn't let me keep him, so I gave it to my grandfather instead. You know I thought that dog looked familiar," Yuri admits and scratches his head.

The girls both groan in disbelief. *They were so close to finding the dog!* "Don't worry," Yuri senses the girls' frustration and realizes he can help them solve the case. "My grandfather owns a mulberry farm not too far from here. If you want to catch up with him, you better hurry," Yuri says as he looks towards a rain cloud in the sky. "If it starts to rain, my grandfather leaves the farm and goes into town to sell his goods. I would take you myself but I have to start my chores," Yuri explains.

He gives them directions to his grandfather's house. The girls thank Yuri before leaving and take off running. They embark on their journey once again, even more excited knowing they are getting closer to completing their mission.

They follow Yuri's directions and arrive at the mulberry farm, just moments before it starts to rain. There, they find Yuri's grandfather, loading his truck, along with the dog that Yuri and his friends had at the market. Kizzy and Nattaya walk over and introduce themselves to him. Kizzy notices that the dog is wearing a dog tag.

They both kneel down and Nattaya turns the dog's tag over. It reads: *Chompoo, royal property of the King of Thailand.* They quickly explain to Yuri's grandfather that the dog belongs to the King of Thailand. The grandfather, pleased to help the girls return the dog, offers them a ride to the King's palace.

When Kizzy and Nattaya arrive at the gates of the King's beautiful palace, the guard refuses to let them in. The guard tells Kizzy and Nattaya that the King is in an important meeting with a guest from the United States.

Kizzy thinks for a moment. "Wait, my dad, General Brown, is here visiting with the King. You have to let us in!" Kizzy proclaims.

"That's right," Nattaya butts in, "and we found Chompoo!," she yells excitedly.

When the guard realizes Kizzy and Nattaya had in fact found the King's missing dog, he hurriedly escorts them to meet with the King. The guard interrupts the King's meeting with General Brown and tells him Kizzy and Nattaya have returned Chompoo.

The King is so excited, that he excuses himself from his meeting with General Brown and rushes out to meet the girls, hoping the news is true. General Brown continues on with the meeting, never realizing his own daughter and her new friend are involved in the rescue of the royal dog.

"How did you find her?" The King asks Kizzy and Nattaya, as he cuddles Chompoo in his arms.

"*HER?*" Both girls look at one another in confusion, as they thought all along that Chompoo was a boy.

"Yes," the King chuckles to himself, recognizing the confused look on the girls' faces.

"Chompoo has been in our family for years, and now she has a family on her own. She just had a litter of newborn puppies and I think I know just how I will reward you for your great efforts in finding her," he tells them. "What are your names?"

Nattaya bows as a sign of respect and then answers the King. "I'm Nattaya Suwan and this is my friend, Kizzy. She's General Brown's daughter, visiting from the U.S."

Kizzy, noticing Nattaya's gesture, also bows to the King before speaking.

"While my dad has been here on assignment, Nattaya and I were on our own mission to find your dog! However, I know my father will be upset once he realizes we interrupted your meeting," Kizzy says nervously.

Impressed by the girls' detective work, the King smiles and thanks them again for returning Chompoo. "I've got to get back to my meeting, but don't worry Kizzy, I won't mention any of this to your father. I'll let you tell him yourself," the King promises Kizzy.

Before he leaves, the King briefly speaks to his guards and arranges for the girls' return home back to the Suwan residence.

MISSION: ACCOMPLISHED

OPERATION PUPPY PATROL

♥ cHOMpOO

A few days later, Kizzy's dad returns to the Suwan home to take Kizzy back to the United States as his mission in Thailand is now complete. As he and Kizzy wave goodbye to the Suwan family, General Brown notices Kizzy has a newborn puppy.

"Kizzy, where did you get that dog?" he asks, unaware that Kizzy was working on a mission of her own.

Kizzy giggles to herself, as she realizes her dad doesn't know that with Nattaya's help, his own daughter was responsible for returning one of the King's most prized possessions back to the royal family. The King had also kept his promise, leaving General Brown to wonder where Kizzy got a new puppy from.

Kizzy smiles and replies, "Oh, it's just a souvenir...from the King of Thailand."

The End

Fun Fact #1: Shih Tzu's are originally from Asia.

- This small dog breed is said to have originated in China, and were apart of royal families for over thousands of years.

Fun Fact #2: In Asia, it is common to be asked to remove your shoes when entering someone's home as a sign of respect.

- This practice originated in Japan, where due to the rainy season, wearing shoes inside of the home could make the floors dirty. Japanese tradition involved eating on tables low to the floor and sleeping on mats on the floor. Due to this tradition, guests and family members begin to leave their shoes in the entryway of the home in order to keep the floors clean.

Fun Fact #3: Silkworms feed on the leaves of mulberry trees.

- Farmers in Thailand grow mulberry trees. The mulberry trees feed silkworms, which create silk that is used to make beautiful silk clothing all over the world.

Fun Fact #4: Muay Thai is a national sport in Thailand.

- Muay Thai, also known as Thai Boxing, is a form of combat sport that originated in Thailand. Muay Thai is a martial arts form that uses fists, elbows, knees, and shins througout the sport.

Fun Fact #5: Thailand has a rainy season.
- Between the months of May and September, rain falls almost every day in Thailand. If you ever get a chance to visit, don't forget your raincoat!